Mary H. Matthew

**Mother's Souvenir**

Composed in the 71st Year of her Age

Mary H. Matthew

**Mother's Souvenir**
*Composed in the 71st Year of her Age*

ISBN/EAN: 9783744652162

Printed in Europe, USA, Canada, Australia, Japan

Cover: Foto ©Andreas Hilbeck / pixelio.de

More available books at **www.hansebooks.com**

# The Soldier's Request.

Liberty's azure scarf
Was mournfully flying
Over a Union Hospital,
Where lay the wounded, sick and dying.

With bayonets they had walled it around.
It must not trail in the dust,
To save her diamond stars
They would die, if they must.

The ladies of the place
Vied with each other,
To amuse and comfort
The sick and dying soldier.

A young lady's special care,
Was brave Albert Corbett;
He was wounded unto death,
And yet he did not know it.

Uncle Sam gets things mixed,
Although he is very kind;
"To get my shirts washed outside,
Say, Miss Jennie, would you mind?"

Now, gentle pity touched my heart;
I thought if it would please a dying soldier,
To have a lady wash his shirts,
Then he shall have that pleasure.

Now, sister, you can see
Why I brought that bundle home
The doctor says he cannot live;
In two or three weeks he will be gone.

When I think of this glorious country,
    That none on earth can match,
And what our brave boys have done for us,
    What of it, if 1 have to scratch?

                                   —M. H. M.

# MOTHER'S SOUVENIR,

Composed in the 71st year of her age.

BY

# MARY H. MATTHEW,

1887.

Griffith & Sons, Publishers, 1035 Howard St.

SAN FRANCISCO.

These poems are dedicated to my children,

  For them to look upon,

That they may remember their Mother

  When she is from them gone.

Mary H. Matthew.

# The Engagement Ring.

## I.

The sparkling of the ring upon my finger
  Caught my mother's eye;
She gave me an earnest look,
  Then breathed a heavy sigh.

## II.

Now mother don't you see,
That ring is the ticket to matrimony;
  See how my sister blushes;
  Off to tell the rest my brother rushes.

### III.

They had higher aims for me,
   Than to marry a mechanic;
They thought I a professor's wife should be—
   I my choice had made and could not see it.

### IV.

Said father: "we might as well consent,
   I know that girl so well,
If she thinks herself right,
   We cannot help ourselves."

### V.

The surface did not trouble me.
   I knew thy noble heart;
They in their kindness could not see,
   That we till death would never part.

## VI.

Calm and quiet in thy mein,
    When oppression called forth thy ire,
Then steadfast in thy duty thou art seen—
    Thine eyes blazing with honest fire.

## VII.

Thou are ever ready to protect,
    The helpless, weak and small;
He stands in conscious virtue great,
    And towers above them all.

## VIII.

Now with all his cares as a man,
    He never adds to mine,
But bears it so manfully,
    And helps me all he can.

## IX.

He nobly the battle fights,
    To win bread for us all,
Against the power of money might–
    The mechanics' chance is small.

## X.

And when bereavement held the cup,
    Of sorrow before our eyes;
Who was it said and pointed up,
    We'll meet him in the skies.

## XI.

Flannel shirt and dirty jacket,
    May cover the golden ore,
Of the deepest thought and feeling—
    Diamonds and velvet vests could do no
    more.

## XII.

Ladies be sure you lift the courteous vail,
 And test your lover's heart;
Or life for you will surely fail,
 Too late you will surely feel the smart.


## XIII.

And when you find the mettle true—
 No matter what garb he wears;
Be sure his arms will shelter you,
 And lighten all your cares.

# My Oldest Daughter.

## I.

God gave me once a treasure,
  Gold could not buy;
It was a little daughter—
  The apple of my eye.

## II.

She gently slipped into a grove,
  Wherever she was wanted;
My darling that I loved—
  My precious oldest daughter.

### III.

Envy and jealousy ne'er swayed her mind,
To all she was gentle and kind;
   She always thought of others good,
   And tried to do just as she should.

### IV.

She would not enter a complaint,
   No matter what they had done;
She always some excuse could make,
   For every erring one.

### V

She was the children's comforter,
   In sorrow or distress;
They went to her for counsel,
   For Hannah knew the best.

## XII.

Then I moved away,
  And left one of my treasures;
She seemed to feel a sister's love,
  Just the same as ever.

## XIII.

Then when on business intent,
To her old home her father went,
  They watched each passing train,
  To see their father's face again.

## XIV.

And when they took him to their home—
How kind was every one;
  When he returned not one forgot,
  Each had a token of forget-me-not.

## XV.

Now in the clouded sky of age,
Another steps upon life's stage,
    Not like her sister in form or face ,
    But just the same in love and grace.

## XVI.

Oh! I have always had my share,
    Of blessings from above:
A tender dove has nestled there,
    We call it household love.

# Johnnie's Request.

## I.

Mamma, take me up now,
  My sister is asleep;
I am tired of playing with my cow,
  She won't stand on her feet.

## II.

His eyes were raised up to my face,
So much like his father's;
  His hands clasped tight my gown,
  How could I put my darling down?

### III.

I glanced around the room—
I do not like disorder.
  How long is this to last I moan,
  And to him sing home, sweet home.


### IV.

A friend of mine just then came in;
Not dressed? are you not going?
  I cannot go to-day, I said,
  And glanced at his weary head.


### V.

Mama, don't go to-day—
  Gity so much bozers;
I won't make a noise at play,
  Nor play with my hosses.

## VI.

May this is a case for Barnum—
　　A lady with a new bonnet,
　　Won't go out to try to show it—
I think I ought to inform him.

## VII.

And as I softly rocked I thought,
　　Love is the wine of woman's life;
Without love her life is naught,
　　All is vexing strife.

## VIII.

He rushed into the room—
In after years, My country calls.
　　My father is too old, my brothers too young—
　　I have inlisted, bless your oldest son.

## IX.

And next, don't shed a tear,
   Think of our great cause;
Mother, I am dying, hear,
   I do not regret the sacrifice.

# The First Passenger Train by Steam Car.

### I.

Fifty-six years ago,
   Some enterprising men,
Started on a trial trip,
   With a fine new engine.

### II.

They must have held their breath,
   As they took their places,
It might be instant death,
   Staring in their face.

### III.

Off the iron colt has started,
  Friends holding their breath;
Oh! if they were only back!
  It looks like sure death.

### IV.

Back they return, looking wise,
  The colors gayly flying;
The stock now would surely rise,
  No need of any dying.

### V.

All honor to that little band,
  That quietly took it through;
And proved what a willing hand,
  And patient brains could do.

## VI.

Now when it goes all through the States,
  I'll sell my patent churns,
Before another fellow wakes,
  Or how to make a fortune learns.

## V II.

An Englishman said "That's an engine,"
It goes very fast and fine:
  The Hinglishman "'Ad that you mind,
  Before I left my 'ome behind."

## VIII.

The poor Indian stood aghast,
  At such an apparation;
They thought it a spirit passed,
  To spread desolation.

## IX.

A Dutchman, through whose land they run,
    Said, " it was hell in harness"
It was to them fine fun—
    They cut his farm in two in earnest.

## X.

A Scotchman said, "Meg is on her mettle,
    She flies through the air;
But barring the witches
    Minds me of Tim O'Shanter's mare.

## XI.

The ladies thought when out of work,
    Handy to go to other places;
Then they looked at each other,
    And said, "Handy to skip the traces."

## XII.

The iron colt is now horse,
　　And nothing his course can stop;
Of the road he is the boss—
　　He takes you to the mountain top.

## XIII.

If you want to feel like a millionaire,
　　Just take a journey for your health;
And go in Pullman's golden car,
　　A journey don't require much wealth.

## XIV.

Now, we have the electric light,
To chase away the shades of night;
　　The telegraph and telephone
　　To bring the absent nearer home.

## XV.

I shoul l not be surprised
To see a train in the skies,
 Drawn by a balloon,
And hear them shout, "all aboard,
 You'll be in China soon."

# Pat's Opinion of American Wars.

## I.

I am going across the water,
   My fortune to seek;
You are are educated, Pat Matthew,
   Be kind enough to speak?

## II.

What was that fight about,
   They had on top that hill?
I'm an ignorant young lout,
   You can tell me if you will.

### III.

It was not the whisky—
 They had not over much—
Nor for the want of wakes
 For they had death's enough.

### IV.

Their huts were separate
 No one touched their stakes;
And plenty of prates to eat.
 Were happy barring the snakes.

### V

There is not another Biddy McGee,
 Acrost the big lake,
To find fault with the corpse,
 When we go to a wake.

## VI.

Things went wrong at home,
   From the west to the east;
So they skipped the big gutter,
   Without ever a priest.


## VII.

Well Tim, you see my lad,
   When they went away,
Forgetting the priest,
   They had no one to pray.


## VIII.

The whisky led them astray,
   In the forest wide;
And no one to pray,
   So alone they died.

## IX.

Then there was Washington,
    Who crossed the raging sea;
And told them to leave the cratere alone,
    And drink only tea.

## X.

And there Tim, my lad you see;
    The king he thought it would be fine
To tax them poor devil's tea,
    To pay for his expensive wine.

## XI.

And then they followed Washington,
    Through mud and rain and snow,
Until they had their tea by tons,
    And made the roaring Lion go.

## XII.

They bound themselves together,
   And called their country States;
Washington was their leader,
   And a president he made.

## XIII.

Some of them had the Nagers,
   The rest did not think it right,
So they wanted to separate.
   And got into a fight.

## XIV.

They had a game rooster,
   His name was U. S. Grant,
He said, "I'll fight all summer
   If that is what you want."

## XV.

It was unconditional surrender,
   No other terms would do;
They forgave each other,
   And swore to the Union to be true.

## XVI.

Hurrah! for the red, white and blue,
   I would sail across the sea, Tim,
In company wid you;
   But (hush) I don't like this tea.

# Tom's Fight at School.

## I.

Grandma, tell me what it is,
   To be a aristocrat;
I can't understand or see,
   What blue blood is, and all that.

## II.

Now the boys are always telling
   Of their old ancestors,
And of their respectabilty.
   What has that to do with us?

### III.

I told them I knew one of their fathers,
 Who was not good, and prove it I could;
Prove it by the Holy Bible—
 I asked them if I should.

### IV.

I claimed him as mine as well as theirs,
 He was no great shakes at that;
His nams was Old Adam,
 "O they said that is too far back."

### V.

Then they said Grandpa
 Was nothing at all;
He sat upon a seat,
 And worked with an awl.

## VI.

Then I thought of my father,
  Whom my grandpa raised—
Who sleeps in the sunny south,
  And fills a soldier's grave.

## VII.

I up and hit that aristocrat,
  And got into a fight;
It ended in two being licked,
  And taking a hasty flight.

## VIII.

I believe that blow I struck,
  Was for freedom from school,
At least they will see,
  Tom Harvey is no longer a fool.

### IX.

Grandma, I saw you turn pale,
  When I in my carelessness,
Let old Grumpy kick the milk
  Over, in the dirt and dust.

### X.

Let me take my father's place,
  And do the best I can—
Let me join in the sacrifice,
  And try to be a man.

### XI.

When my father died,
  Old grandpa took us all;
He, his children kept,
  By tugging with an awl.

## XII.

I kr o·v I shall be expelled,
  Straightway, from the school;
It will be all for the best,
  We will see when we are cool.


## XIII.

I'll sit down on the bench,
  And work through the day,
And go to school at night,
  For your sake give up play.


## XIV.

You stint yourself in everything,
  To help us aleng,
To get an education,
  And make us good and strong.

## XV.

Oh! grandma what have I done,
  You are surely crying;
To take the place of your son,
  Is there any harm in trying?


## XVI.

I'll work on grandpa's seat,
  Until I earn a better one,
Perhaps a judge's bench,
  Awaits your Harry's Son.

# My Creed.

### I.

I take the Bible for my guide,
   And let all creeds alone;
Creeds are by man supplied,
   The Bible, God's alone.

### II.

No Babtist can be washed,
   In pools or rivers, clean,
No Methodist by hell be scorched,
   If by the Bible light his works are seen.

## III.

No Presbyterian in Heaven can shine,
   Although he be elected;
Unless he shapes his life by book divine,
   He will not be expected.


## IV.

Now we will take the Quaker plain,
Who keeps in sight his honest fame,
   And thinks no harm to cheat in trade,
   And says he by the spirit prayed.


## V

Ye power loving priests,
   Have ye not overshot the word,
And received from bended knees,
   The homage only due your God?

## VI.

Some say we all, to Heaven will go,
   Christs blood atones for all,
   As easy as school boys ride down hill,
With sleds on ice and snow.


## VII.

O, give me just my Bible then,
Away with all the creeds of man;
   I find within its holy light,
   The sure guide to all thats right.

# The Selfish Man.

## I.

Beware of a thorough selfish man,
　The world began and ends with him.
He will deceive you if he can,
　To serve himself is ne'er a sin.

## II.

True friendship long cannot live,
　With a thorough selfish one;
He exacts all and nothing gives,
　He cannot see the right from wrong.

### III.

But let him have an ax to grind;
   How different he can be;
And when he has gained his point,
   Then how supercilious, you must see.

### IV.

He grinds beneath his selfish will,
   The hearts he ought to cherish:
They find that he a tyrant is,
   And must succumb or perish.

### V

And when he gets the inside track,
   Another name for cheating,
He does not even pity him,
   His fraud has sorely beaten.

## VI.

Workingmen are his common prey,
  He has a right to what they earn—
He is made of better clay than they,
  And calls himself a gentleman.

## VII.

No power on earth can stop the selfish tide,
  Unless he believes in the power of God,
And that for him a Saviour died,
  Then bends beneath his chastening rod.

# Look to God alone for your Reward.

## I.

To do the best you can,
  And then to be blamed at last;
Appears to be the lot of man,
  Its my experience in the past.

## II.

Blind to all the faults you see
  In those you love so well,
And find for you no charity,
  It grieves me sore to tell.

### III.

To sacrifice your worldly all,
  And think it not o'er dear;
Then see your hoped for castles fall,
  Without from them a sigh or tear.

### IV.

To have your little ones your own,
Until they are to manhood grown,
  Then waver in their love,
  Because by other's influence drove.

### V

And when the cords of love unbind,
  And you have cast them off;
How sweet the master's words so kind,
  Look for true happiness aloft.

# Grandma's Story for Nellie.

## THE REBELLIOUS COAL SCUTTLE.

### I.

Come, Nellie, I will tell you,
    What a naughty scuttle did;
How it began a rebellion,
    And threw your Grandma on her head.

### II.

My friend, Mrs. Lawson,
    Had to move away;
Her husband's business called them,
    They could no longer stay.

### III.

She left me some household things
   She could not take along;
Amongst them was a scuttle,
   Gayly painted, and very strong.

### IV.

Every time I tried to pass,
   There was opposition,
Until I called him to account,
   And found out the true position.

### V

I had before his advent,
   A true and worthy servant,
Who understood just what I meant,
   And to do his duty was content.

## VI.

It was a sawed off oil can,
  That had served me so long;
Scuttle would not take his place,
  Which I thought very wrong.


## VII.

At last the monitor was consulted,
  And moved out from the wall,
And allowed the scuttle insulted,
  His fancied privileges all.


## VIII.

Under the stove he would not be,
  But stood his ground outside;
He was dressed too nice you see,
  And felt above sawed off beside.

## IX.

Now don't you think old sawed off,
  Of the two the best?
He never tripped poor Grandma,
  But to please her did his best.

# Little Maggie.

### I.

Two years ago a little bird.
  Fluttered in my door,
I's in the way, I'se come to play,
  Mamma is at the store.

### II.

God bless this little child I said,
  She is trying to help her mother,
By trusting her little self,
  To the care of another.

### III.

How thankful mothers ought to be,
  Whose husband's can provide,
That they may always see,
  Their children at their side.

### IV.

She would romp and play,
With all the rest,
  As happy as a lark,
  Toward night she'd say, its most dark.

### V

One day she was doing something wrong,
I said Margaret in an angry tone,
  Now, said she, I know you're mad,
  My name is only little Mag.

## VI.

The mysteries of relationship,
   Was to her a puzzle,
If I was grandma to the rest
   Why was I not to her?

## VII.

One day she meddled with the dough,
Now grandma don't you know,
   I heard you a lady tell,
   Babies must be 'numbered when not well.

## VIII.

'Sides I have to make pies,
   And learn to 'took more,
I's going to make apple-sauce,
   While mamma's in the store.

## IX.

I wanted to slap her,
   Sometimes, as I did my own,
Then I would think to myself,
   Poor baby, her father is dead and gone.


## X.

They said that I spoiled her,
   I expect that I did.
I could not correct her
   The precious little kid.

# Decoration Day.

### I.

A picture hung in the parlor,
  Of an oldest son,
He died in the army,
  He was a well beloved one.

### II.

It was Decoration day,
  All looked sorrowful and sad,
Even the children could not play,
  Poor grandma felt so bad.

### III.

A crowning wreath was made,
    Each one a flower brought,
Ah! I knew what it said,
    It was an emblem of the thought.


### IV.

A wreath of mourning cypress
    Proclaimed the conflict passed,
The brave heroes are dead,
    And peace is gained at last.


### V

Canterberrybell, I love the still,
    Proclaim a sister's love,
The flowering almond hope,
    I'll meet thee above.

## VI.

Our country was calling
  Her boys to her aid,
To save her from separation,
  And a rebel raid.

## VII.

He went at the summons,
  And gave up his life,
To quiet the rebellion,
  And end the fierce strife.

## VIII.

He did not regret
  The steps he had taken,
But thought it a glory,
  To die for this nation.

.

## IX.

He died in a southern land,
  Ah! how sad for me to tell,
With his furlough in his hand,
  He said, "God doeth all things well."

## X.

Oh! this is Decoration day,
  No loving hands are near,
Oh! will some gentle loving hand.
  Drop on his grave a rose or tear?

# What Carrie Missed.

## I.

God took a loving mother,
　　Unto the spirit side,
She had to leave them all,
　　Her comforter and pride.

## II.

Four year old Carrie came and said,
　　"Aunty, where is my mamma?
　　Is she in the parlor?
Papa says she's dead."

### III.

Carrie let me rock you,
　　As your mamma did;
I'll tell you a pretty story,
　　And put you in your crib.

### IV.

Yes, aunty I'll go to you,
　　And let you sing me asleep—
If you will only let me have
　　Of mamma just a little peep.

### V

I took her in the room,
　　Where lay all that was left,
Of that loving mother
　　Of whose care she was bereft.

## VI.

She stooped down and kissed her,
  Then in great surprise,
Oh! Auntie, where is the rest of mamma?
  And tears stood in her eyes.


## VII

A little child shall lead you,
  So our Saviour said,
I wondered where we'd be,
  Oh! where, when we are dead?


## VIII.

She missed the return,
  Of her loving caress,
She knew something was wrong,
  Her mamma was not so remiss.

## IX.

The brow may be fair,
   The eyes may be bright,
But if the soul is missing,
   All is dark as night,

# The Bride's Reply.

## I.

It was the month of January,
  The thaw had begun;
Niagara River was full of ice,
  That glistened in the sun.

## II.

Passengers had been delayed,
  They could not get across,
No matter what the consequences,
  Nor how much the loss.

### III.

A moving mass of broken ice,
    Swept swiftly along;
"No boat could live in that," they said,
    "No matter how staunch or strong."

### IV.

A man arrived upon the scene,
    A young girl by his side;
"My time is up," he  said,
    "I must reach the other side."

### V

One to the lady said,
    "Have you from home ran away,
That he is so anxious to cross,
    By the light of this day?"

### VI.

The insult your words imply;
　　This is no time to resent;
It is true, I have left my home,
　　But with my parents consent.

### VII.

Come boatman, man the oars,
　　And let us haste away,
Your lives I will insure,
　　And give you double pay.

### VIII.

"Say Jack, I'm going across,
　　Won't you go along?
The young man says he will pilot us;
　　We won't be less courageous than the girl.

## IX.

The danger lay in freezing fast,
   And losing the boat's control;
Then into the lake we will go,
   And perish every soul.

## X.

He had taken a view,
   Of the currents of the river;
And was sure he could cross this morn,
   Just as well as ever.

## XI.

Lake Erie's ice was running fast,
   Straight up the winding river,
It seemed a formidable pass,
   To those who wished to go over.

## XII.

We took our seats in the boat,
　Ten being our number,
Among'st boat hooks, and ropes,
　The crowd gazing in wonder

## XIII.

Two miles above the landing.
　We were forced to go;
It was very dangerous,
　Also very slow.

## XIV.

Down four miles more we came,
　Through the center of the river,
Before striking the current,
　That would take us safely over.

## XV.

We had been three hours,
  Slowly working our way;
On landing, we were greeted,
  With a loud, "Hurrah!"


## XVI.

"Say lady, please to tell us,
  Why you was so calm,
It appeared very dangerous,
  Was you not dreading harm?"


## XVII.

"We started on our voyage
  Through life, a few hours before;
Now was the chance to show him,
  I would stand by his side ever more.

## XVIII.

I knew he was expected,
    At a certain time:
He should keep his word with men,
    Without any hindrance of mine.

## XIX.

I knew he had begun the race
    For truth and honor among men;
What could a loyal wife do,
    But go with him then?

# The Lord's Prayer.

## I.

Did it ever occur to you
    How all sufficient it can be.
If you only in earnest true,
    Humbly bend the supplicating knee.

## II.

Sweet, the name of our Father
    That calls us all to Him;
He is our Redeemer,
    And saves us all from sin.

## IX.

Guard us from evil,
  For thou hast the power;
From sin and the devil,
  We are in danger every hour.


## X.

It will give you light to see
  What a child of God's should be;
And, if you have grief to meet
  Lay it at your Father's feet.